STEP INTO READING® will help your child get there. The program offers five steps to reading success. Each step includes fun stories and colorful art or photographs. In addition to original fiction and books with favorite characters, there are Step into Reading Non-Fiction Readers, Phonics Readers and Boxed Sets, Sticker Readers, and Comic Readers—a complete literacy program with something to interest every child.

Learning to Read, Step by Step!

Ready to Read   Preschool–Kindergarten
• big type and easy words • rhyme and rhythm • picture clues
For children who know the alphabet and are eager to begin reading.

Reading with Help   Preschool–Grade 1
• basic vocabulary • short sentences • simple stories
For children who recognize familiar words and sound out new words with help.

Reading on Your Own   Grades 1–3
• engaging characters • easy-to-follow plots • popular topics
For children who are ready to read on their own.

Reading Paragraphs   Grades 2–3
• challenging vocabulary • short paragraphs • exciting stories
For newly independent readers who read simple sentences with confidence.

Ready for Chapters   Grades 2–4
• chapters • longer paragraphs • full-color art
For children who want to take the plunge into chapter books but still like colorful pictures.

STEP INTO READING® is designed to give every child a successful reading experience. The grade levels are only guides; children will progress through the steps at their own speed, developing confidence in their reading.

Remember, a lifetime love of reading starts with a single step!

For my grandma Mabel Owen, with love.
And for Mom, grandma to Joey and Audrey.
—F.G.

For Zoe, the chosen one
—S.D.

Visit us on the Web!
StepIntoReading.com
rhcbooks.com

Educators and librarians, for a variety of teaching tools, visit us at RHTeachersLibrarians.com

Library of Congress Cataloging-in-Publication Data
Names: Gilbert, Frances, author. | DiCicco, Sue, illustrator.
Title: I love my grandma! / by Frances Gilbert ; illustrated by Sue DiCicco.
Description: First edition. | New York : Random House Children's Books, [2020] | Summary:
"A girl and her grandmother bike and play games, read and have tea parties, and reminisce about
Grandma's own grandmother." —Provided by publisher.
Identifiers: LCCN 2019010398 | ISBN 978-0-593-12340-9 (trade pbk.) |
ISBN 978-0-593-12339-3 (library binding) | ISBN 978-0-593-12338-6 (ebook)
Subjects: | CYAC: Grandmothers—Fiction.
Classification: LCC PZ7.1.G547 Iah 2020 | DDC [E]—dc23

Printed in the United States of America
10 9 8 7 6 5 4 3 2 1

I Love My Grandma!

by Frances Gilbert
illustrated by Sue DiCicco

Random House 🏠 New York

This is my mom.

I love my mom!

My mom
has a mom, too.

My mom's mom
is my grandma.

I love my grandma!

At my house,
we make
pizzas together.

At Grandma's house,
we drink tea
from fancy cups.

On sunny days,
we ride our bikes
in the park.

On rainy days,
we listen to music
and dance.

On snowy days,
we make
snow angels!

When Grandma
babysits me,
we watch movies
and eat popcorn.

When I babysit
Grandma,
we play games
and eat cupcakes.

Grandma reads books
to me.

And I read books
to Grandma.

I am a good reader,
and so is Grandma!

I love to look in
Grandma's purse.
I find candy,

coins,

a mirror,

a comb,

a red lipstick,

and photos of me!

Grandma shows me
photos of her
when she was
a little girl!

My grandma
had a
grandma, too!

My grandma's
grandma
loved to make pizzas,

read books,

dance,

and make snow angels!

Grandmas are the best!

And the best thing about my grandma is— <u>she</u> loves <u>me</u>!